The Doll's House

Jean Maye

Mouse Chased Cat
Publications

DEDICATION

The Doll's House is dedicated to my late Auntie Joyce, whose laughter made all things possible and who bequeathed one of her much-loved doll's houses to me. It was her doll's house that inspired this story.

ACKNOWLEDGMENTS

With thanks to Hilary Wright, Ruth Tofield for their editing advice.

Also, special thanks to Tom Boon for the final editing and proofreading for this publication.

1

Ever since Inga and Matt Taylor adopted Sienna, six months ago, when she was seven, she had been allowed to explore everywhere in her new home apart from Anika's bedroom. To go into this room, she needed to ask permission – and even then, either Matt or Inga would supervise her.

Sienna liked to stand and study the beautifully decorated bedroom. She felt sorry for the fluffy toys, especially her favourite, the moose – arranged on the pink cushioned armchair and resting against the pillows and fairy duvet, as if they were waiting to be played with. Then her big brown eyes would wander across the room, past the dressing table with its mirror and little stool. On the opposite side of the room was a tall cupboard. It was quite an ordinary sort of cupboard with doors and a keyhole, but no key. It was always kept locked. The locked cupboard was the only thing she wasn't allowed to explore, and she didn't understand why.

Whenever she was in Anika's bedroom, Sienna couldn't help but wonder what mysterious event had taken Inga and Matt's only five-year-old daughter away from them, four years ago. She longed to know more about Anika but had never dared to ask.

After a few minutes of soaking up the atmosphere and mystery of the room, Inga or Matt, whoever was with her at the time, would say in a broken voice, 'That's enough, now, Sienna,' and lead her out before closing the door behind them.

Sienna would constantly be asking herself questions: Why had Anika gone missing without a trace? Had she run away? Maybe she hadn't liked living with the Taylors. It couldn't be much fun to have your parents lock the cupboard in your own room. *I mean, what fun is that?*

Devonshire Cottage was not a small house, nor unusually large, but its layout made it seem bigger and interesting.

At the top of the large carpeted staircase was the family bathroom. Two corridors led away from it in opposite directions, with two bedrooms down each. Sienna particularly liked this, because her bedroom was situated away from the Taylors', and they had made the next-door bedroom into a playroom for her. It was like having her own private wing of the house. Anika's old bedroom was next to her mum and dad's room.

Inga and Matt had talked openly about their only child's disappearance in a meeting they had with the social worker and Sienna soon after she had moved in. They explained to her that it was important for her to know that she would be safe living with them, and that children rarely went missing these days without being found. They could have kept this information a secret from her, but all the adults believed it was best she knew from the start of them living together as a family, rather than to find out later from anyone else.

'But why did she run away?' asked Sienna. 'And why didn't she come back?'

At the time, Sienna was not only intrigued as to

where Anika had vanished to, but she also wanted to know what type of behaviour and rules the Taylors had. If they were bad or too restrictive, then this could have been the reason why Anika had run away.

Sienna had given Anika's disappearance much thought and wondered why social services even considered a place for her to live where children simply 'disappeared'. She'd had enough challenges in her young life already since that devastating day three years ago when her parents' light aircraft crashed off the coast of Scarborough. After that, she was sent to live with Mrs Cooper, a very large, robust foster carer. Usually, she would only foster children on an emergency basis, but Sienna remembered her saying 'This child needs stability now,' so social services agreed that Sienna could stay until a permanent family was found.

As it turned out, Mrs Cooper was an exceedingly kind woman who had devoted her life to fostering after the death of her husband eighteen years ago, so she also knew about loss and grief. At first, Sienna did not talk about losing her parents, but she found so much comfort in Mrs Cooper's friendly face, and the way in which she spoke helped Sienna feel at ease. Later, Sienna visited a counsellor called Isabella who was also lovely. There she sometimes played with toys whilst they chatted, which she loved.

Sienna's feelings were mixed when she left Mrs Cooper's home to go and live with Inga and Matt. Sadness that she probably would not see Mrs Cooper again, and anxiety because she had no idea what it might be like living with the Taylors, even though she'd met them on several occasions. It was only when she was packing to leave Mrs Cooper's that a flood of excitement swept through her, as she thought what the future could hold!

When she arrived outside the front door of the Taylors, 'supposedly' her new parents, she thought of her own mum and dad. She missed them so much and could feel tears welling up, but bravely fought them back. At that moment, she did not believe that she could ever be happy or laugh again.

2

Six months later, and about an hour ago, Sienna had quietly sneaked into Matt's office and stolen the key to Anika's cupboard from the top drawer of his desk. Earlier that morning she had been in his office showing him a picture that she had drawn of Richmond Castle, close to where they lived. Matt always loved her drawings but as he thanked her and happily pinned it onto his cork notice board, together with other pictures she had drawn the phone rang. A pressing matter at work meant that he had to leave in a rush, and she noticed he had forgotten to lock his desk drawer. The place she knew where the key to Anika's cupboard was kept.

Although she knew it was wrong to take something which wasn't hers, the suspense of finding out what was in the cupboard was too much to bear. All she had to do was to get into Anika's bedroom, unlock the cupboard and take a peek. Then, without anyone knowing, she would lock it again and place the key back in the drawer. Simple! Absolutely nothing could go wrong!

Or could it?

The cooking apples in their small garden orchard had grown earlier than expected this summer, which Inga put down to climate change. She still had stewed apples that she had frozen from the other apple tree varieties last autumn. Because of this,

Inga was busy in the kitchen making apple pies, an apple cake and sauces.

Sienna didn't like apples very much, so she saw no joy in helping. But also, with the key to the cupboard now safely in her pocket, it was a prime time to go exploring.

So, when Inga asked her if she wanted to help, Sienna screwed her nose up and said, 'I would rather play upstairs,' then twirled strands of her wavy thick black hair between her fingers.

'Okay,' Inga smiled and began peeling another apple, 'But only for a short while because the rain is going to clear soon, and the fresh air will do you good.'

Making certain Inga was fully occupied with her baking, Sienna went upstairs, crept along the landing, and slid into Anika's bedroom. Her heart was racing in anticipation.

She stood in front of the forbidden cupboard. Her fist was closed tight around the key hidden in her pocket. Now she felt bad about stealing the key, but she had to know why this cupboard was locked. Maybe there was a clue inside to Anika's disappearance?

She put her head on one side, listening intently to Inga downstairs, but all she could hear was the electric mixer which sounded to her like an aeroplane engine whining as it crashed into the North Sea... She shuddered. *Best not to think about that.*

Pull yourself together. The noise would work to her advantage. Inga wouldn't be able to hear her moving about upstairs and wonder what she was doing. And even if she got found out, what was the worst that could happen? All they would do was tell her off and send her to her room. They couldn't possibly think about sending her away – or could they?

As adrenaline surged through her body, she quickly pulled out the key and turned the lock – CLICK!

Of all things, Sienna had not expected to find a doll's house hidden in the cupboard. She stared up at it. It was beautiful! It had perfect miniature windows and oh, what a wonderful little front door, such a bright red colour. How she wished she could see inside. It reminded her of Mrs Cooper's red front door when she had first arrived. That had seemed enormous at the time, but at four years old, everything then looked bigger than it really was.

Now she trembled with delight and adrenaline ran through her veins, so much so that she was almost feeling sick. She was utterly transfixed by the tiny front door, the most delightful front door she'd ever seen!

She had to get the doll's house out. But how? The shelf it was on was too high to reach. Standing on tiptoe, Sienna reached up to try to open the front door. If she could at least do that, then perhaps she could peep inside. But it was still too high.

She fetched the stool from Anika's dressing table, climbed onto it and reached out again to the red panelled door. This time she could just about reach. But just as her fingers gently pressed against the doll's house front door, the bedroom door burst open behind her and there stood Inga, looking very cross indeed.

The shock of being found out made Sienna lose her balance and she toppled off the stool onto the carpet with a thud. Inga rushed over to her and helped her up.

'Have you hurt yourself?'

Sienna shook her head, feeling sorry for herself. Inga took Sienna's hand and helped her up and they sat on the bed looking up at the doll's house.

'The doll's house was locked away for a reason, Sienna,' said Inga. 'It belonged to Anika, and...'

Sienna had frequently felt miserable since the death of her parents, but now she felt her entire body fill up with both guilt and sadness. Blood rushed to her face, and tears filled her eyes. Inga put her arms around her, and Sienna found herself leaning against her.

'I'm sorry Anika went away. I wish she would come back. Then I'd have someone to play with.'

'Matt and I would love that to happen. Then you'd be sisters.'

'But why can't I play with the doll's house?'

Inga looked at the doll's house then back at Sienna. 'Anika was playing with the doll's house when she disappeared. At least we thought she was, but she must have gone outside to play and forgot to tell us.'

'So, an evil man snatched her!' exclaimed Sienna.

'We don't know. But she would never have left us willingly. That is why doing what adults say and telling the truth is so important.' Inga ran her fingers through Sienna's hair. 'Come on, give me a hand downstairs and I'll talk to Matt this evening about letting you play with the doll's house.'

Inga closed the cupboard door. 'How did you open the cupboard without the key?'

Then she spotted the key in the lock. 'How did you get the key?' Sienna looked down in shame.

'Promise me you won't ever take something that does not belong to you again. Do you understand?'

Sienna nodded. But she could not look at Inga. How could she make a promise like that? The world was too full of mysteries to make promises about not taking keys to solve them. Besides, there must be so many adventures to go on – adventures that were unlikely to include grown-ups and strict rules.

3

There was an unusual amount of silence during supper. Pasta bake was one of Sienna's favourites, but that evening the pasta seemed hard to swallow until she washed it down with a gulp of orange squash.

Sienna's eyes wandered over to a scrumptious looking apple cake resting on a one of the kitchen units. If she wasn't in so much trouble, or feeling so sick with anticipation, she did think she could be tempted to try a little.

Although Inga gave Sienna a reassuring smile, it did not make her feel any better. She was fed up with Matt looking so angry, so she placed her fork on the plate and pushed back her chair.

'Where do you think you're off to?' demanded Matt. 'Sit down. There are things we need to discuss.'

'I was going to my room.' She slumped back onto her chair, her face as glum as it could be.

Matt glared at her intensely. 'Stealing is not acceptable. It doesn't matter what you want or what you think you need, you don't steal it, you ask for it. Those are the rules here and I imagine in every other house!'

Sienna had not seen him frown like that before. If she hadn't been in so much trouble she would have laughed, because his bushy eyebrows looked like wriggling caterpillars. But she knew she needed to be as solemn as he was. 'I'm sorry. I promise never to do it again.'

Matt kept a stern face for a few minutes as they all sat in silence. Then he let out a big sigh. 'Okay, we'll put the doll's house in your playroom, Sienna. How about that?

Sienna rushed to Matt and gave him a big hug and he and Inga smiled.

After supper, as he promised, Matt moved the doll's house into the playroom and Sienna sat in front of it, admiring the beautiful red panelled front door. She carefully pushed open the front to look inside and immediately gasped with delight. It was simply sumptuous!

The doll's house had four rooms to the front: two upstairs and two down. Each of the windows had colourful curtains. The downstairs room on the left was a sitting room with a fireplace, two armchairs, a settee and pictures on the wall. She realised with surprise that it looked very like the Taylors' lounge downstairs.

The downstairs room on the right was like another lounge, but in it was a perfect, miniature grand piano with the top propped open, just like a real grand piano in a music room. Eager to see if the piano worked, Sienna lifted the lid and tried the little white and black keys. Although the keys moved, no sound came out. She wondered what it would be like to be able to play a real piano. Perhaps one day she might be able to learn.

She peered into the upstairs bedrooms, two at the front, one at the back. There was a bathroom next to the back bedroom with a gorgeous roll-top bath. The whole house was luxurious, intriguing, beautiful. 'How could Anika even think about leaving this doll's house and prefer to play outside?' she muttered to herself.

Smiling, Inga popped her head around the door. 'It's bedtime.' Sienna pulled a face. Inga held out her hand.

'Come on, there's a few more weeks of summer

holidays before you go back to school. Plenty of time to play with the doll's house.'

Sienna scowled. Why did Inga have to spoil things by mentioning school? She stormed out and stomped into her bedroom where she reluctantly started getting ready for bed.

A little while later, Inga walked in and tucked her into bed making sure she was comfortable.

'Sienna,' she said softly, 'We understand life has been difficult for you.'

She looked at the framed photograph of Sienna with her birth mum and dad resting on Sienna's bedside cabinet next to her lamp.

'We can never replace your birth mum and dad and would not want to, but we are your parents now. We'll be here for you and love you no matter what.' She kissed Sienna on the cheek.

Deep down, Sienna knew the Taylors loved her, and part of her wanted to hug Inga there and then, but she couldn't quite manage it. She just nodded appreciatively and turned away.

It wasn't long before she fell asleep and dreamed she was on stage in a large concert hall, wearing a fine evening dress and playing the grand piano from the doll's house.

It was piano music that woke her. Sienna sat up, still half asleep, and listened to the catchy tune for a moment. Thinking she was still dreaming, she lay back down and tried to pick up the same dream, but the music just got louder and louder.

She switched on her bedside lamp, flung back the duvet and put on her dressing gown and slippers. Quietly opening her bedroom door, she listened intently. The music seemed to be coming from her playroom. *Perhaps Inga or Matt woke in the night and decided to fix the piano for me?* she thought.

She hurried excitedly to the playroom, but as soon as she opened the door and turned the light on, the music instantly stopped.

What's going on? she thought and peered through the window of the doll's house into the music room. Everything was as she had left it. Again, she tried the piano keys, but there was still no sound. Puzzled, she turned out the light and went back to bed. The rest of that night she tossed and turned, the piano music playing endlessly in her head.

Where had the music come from?

In the morning, she would ask Inga and Matt if they had been playing piano music in the middle of the night, and they would say 'yes', and everything would be all right.

Or would it?

4

Sienna went downstairs the next morning to find
Inga making apple pancakes for breakfast. Sienna
loved pancakes. But apple sauce? Yuck! She didn't
fancy this at all. But there was something about the
hot sugary cinnamon smell that enticed her to try
one. It made her tongue tingle and was so delicious
that she almost forgot to ask Inga and Matt about
the piano music in the night. It was only when she
scooped up the last mouthful of pancake that she
remembered.

'I liked the piano music in the night,' ventured Sienna.

Matt raised his bushy eyebrows at Inga and
poured them both another mug of coffee.

'I said I liked the piano music last night,' Sienna
repeated, shifting forward in her seat in anticipation

for an answer.

'There was no one playing music in the night here,' said Matt firmly. Sienna's face flushed, simmering in frustration.

'Perhaps it was in a passing car?' she suggested without believing this herself.

Inga looked puzzled. 'We're a long way from the main road.'

'Well I don't think it was a passing car anyway!' Sienna exclaimed defiantly. 'It was definitely playing in this house! Why don't you believe me? My mum and dad would have believed me!'

In fury, she got up from the table and stomped out into the garden, leaving both Inga and Matt looking hurt and upset.

It was rather chilly outside today for summer and although she was red-hot angry, it made her shiver. She stomped into the orchard area of the garden and stared at the ground below the apple trees. She wished she was tall enough to reach one of the growing apples on a tree so she could pick it and throw it to get rid of some of her anger. Instead, she kicked a stump of grass with her foot and watched as some ants marched out from underneath.

Sienna often felt angry since her parents died, but as she turned back towards the house, she wondered why she felt so much anger towards the Taylors. As she had told the social worker, she liked them from the first day she met them. Sometimes she lay in bed at night and thought how loving, kind, and considerate they were to her. Most of all, how well they coped with her moods.

Sometimes she thought about calling them mum and dad, but the idea made her feel like she was betraying her parents. And if she had told her parents she'd heard piano music in the middle of the night, or anything else for that matter, they would have believed her. She pondered for a moment then looked up to the sky and shouted tearfully, 'Life just isn't fair!'

She went back inside.

Matt smiled. 'Why don't you give Jenny a ring and see if she wants to come and play? I could go and pick her up.'

'She's gone to her grandparents for the rest of the holidays,' Sienna replied in a sulky voice.

Jenny had been the first girl who greeted Sienna at her new school, and they got on straight away. But Jenny came from a big family, so she always had somewhere exciting to go during the school holidays.

Suddenly Sienna had an idea which cheered her up.

'Can I make little fairy cakes to put in the kitchen of the doll's house?'

'Of course, we can,' said Inga.

'What a good idea!' said Matt. He kissed Inga on the cheek and picked up his car keys then ruffled Sienna's hair in his hands and winked at his wife.

'See you later, ladies.'

'Have a good day,' replied Inga with a smile.

'I'm sure I will, but I'd rather be counting fairy cakes than preparing other people's business accounts.' He blew them a kiss and left.

'Well, now,' said Inga, 'I have plenty of icing sugar and food colouring so we can make lots of different colours if you like.'

Sienna's face flushed with joy. Soon she and Inga were busy mixing ingredients and getting flour in their hair. Not only that, when Sienna looked at her hands, she also had green fingers from the food colouring.

She raised her hand wiggling her fingers for Inga to see. Inga laughed and wiped away the flour from her hair then she smudged a streak of blue food colouring right across her own cheeks.

Sienna couldn't remember when she had laughed so much making cakes. Indeed, she couldn't remember the last time she had laughed so much at all.

Trying to cut the cakes small enough to fit on the kitchen table in the doll's house was nearly impossible, but they managed it. Sienna took the tiny fairy cakes to the playroom and delicately placed three on the miniature kitchen table, two yellow and one pink, each with a delicate ready-made iced flower on the top. Next time Jenny came over, Sienna would take great pleasure in showing her the doll's house.

As soon as Sienna was satisfied with the arrangement of the cakes in the doll's house, she went back downstairs to eat some of the full-sized ones.

'I really did hear piano music,' said Sienna, her

mouth full of cake.

Inga sipped her tea. 'We had a piano a few years ago. Anika was having lessons. Two years after she disappeared, we sold it. That's why we made a music room in the doll's house, it was her favourite room to play with.'

'I wish you'd kept the real piano. I'd love to learn how to play a piano.'

'That was before we even thought about adopting, Sienna. Besides, it was too much of a reminder.'

'I suppose so, but I did like the music last night.'

Inga smiled, 'Sometimes dreams can feel real. They are very powerful and can leave you confused. If you hear the music again, come and get me and I'll come and investigate with you.'

Sienna gave Inga a great big hug.

5

At bedtime Inga went into the playroom with Sienna and checked out the room. Sienna looked around carefully, making sure everything was as she had left it. The three miniature fairy cakes sat untouched on the doll's house kitchen table. Satisfied, she went to bed. Inga tucked her in, kissed her on the forehead and wished her sweet dreams.

When the piano music woke her, Sienna could not remember what she had been dreaming about or if she had been dreaming at all. Without even bothering with her dressing gown and slippers, she rushed along the corridor to Inga and Matt's bedroom as Inga had told her to do.

'The piano music is playing!' she shouted. 'Come quickly!'

Both Inga and Matt sat up with a jerk.

Sienna ran down the corridor to the playroom and flung open the door, but the music immediately stopped and all she saw was the darkness of the night.

Inga held out her hand to Sienna. She took it, glad of the reassurance. Matt switched on the light and walked in. 'There's nothing here, and no one is playing any music.'

'But there was music! I heard it!'

'Perhaps you just had another weird dream,' said Inga.

'I'm going back to bed,' said Matt. 'I suggest we all do the same. Come on, young lady. I'll tuck you in, just to make sure there's not a piano player hidden in your room.' Sienna knew he was trying to be kind, but she wished he believed her.

She took a last look inside the doll's house – and gasped. 'Someone's eaten a fairy cake!' She pulled free from Matt and ran over to the doll's house.

'And who do you think has eaten it?' asked Matt.

Sienna looked at the other toys in the room: three teddies, two dolls and a moose. The moose had been her favourite until the doll's house, and she often cuddled up to him in bed.

Inga picked up the moose and gave it to Sienna. 'Perhaps you should take moose to bed with you.'

'I'll check the room in the morning for mice,' said Matt. 'If we have them in the attic again, one may have sneaked in here.'

'Yes, and eaten the fairy cake and played on the doll's house grand piano!' Sienna exclaimed in fury. She grabbed the moose and stormed out of the room.

Back in her bedroom, she climbed into bed, and Matt sat with her until she closed her eyes. But as soon as he tiptoed out of the room, Sienna opened her eyes and sprang out of bed. If the grown-ups didn't believe her, she'd keep watch in the playroom all night.

The next morning Inga found her curled up fast asleep on the playroom floor cuddling up to the moose. Inga covered her with a blanket and eased a pillow under her head, glancing quizzically at the doll's house.

When Sienna woke, her body felt stiff from sleeping on the floor. She pushed away the cover, stretched her arms and legs out like a starfish, then rubbed them.

The sun was shining through the gap in the curtains. She pulled them back revealing the sunny garden outside and smiled. But as she walked past the doll's house to go to the bathroom, she froze in disbelief... the two remaining fairy cakes had also vanished!

6

That whole morning Sienna was tired and irritable. She felt stiff from sleeping on the floor and frustrated that someone or something had stolen the other two fairy cakes. Matt had set mouse-friendly traps, but Sienna felt sure they were dealing with something more sinister than a mouse.

'Come into Richmond with me,' said Inga. Usually, Sienna would have jumped at the chance, but her mind was on other things.

'I don't want to. It's boring and I have a mystery here to solve.'

'Well, I fancy toasted tea-cakes and a pot of tea from Jolly's Tea Shop,' said Inga, knowing this was something Sienna just couldn't refuse.

'Oh,' mused Sienna, thinking about Jolly's

delicious hot chocolate, 'I suppose I could come for a little while.'

So, they drove the mile through the Yorkshire Dales into Richmond town with Sienna staring out of the window at the drystone walls and expanses of purple heather on the moorland. All the time her thoughts were still very much on the mystery of the piano playing and the missing fairy cakes.

That day the castle was having an event, so they saw lots of people dressed in strange multi-coloured medieval costumes. Some looked quite extraordinary, and on another day she might have laughed, but Sienna wasn't in the mood today.

Inga and Sienna browsed around a few shops and soon found themselves inside the quirky Jolly's Tea Shop, their favourite café. Sienna enjoyed looking around at the multitude of colourful teapots displayed on the shelves and watching the other customers already munching a glorious choice of cakes and scones. They sat by the window at a little round table that had a pretty tablecloth decorated with daisies.

Soon they were tucking into delicious tea cakes

dripping with butter and Sienna's favourite, a rich hot chocolate drink with thick cream floating on the top.

'I do like it here,' announced Sienna suddenly. 'And thank you for the teacakes and hot chocolate!' She wiped chocolate froth from her mouth with a serviette.

'You're welcome,' said Inga with a warm loving smile.

'Hello Sienna. You're becoming one of my most regular customers!' Before they knew it Mrs Polly Jolly, the owner of the tea shop, was standing beside them with her cherry-red cheeks and a wide smile.

'Hello,' replied Sienna. 'I think your tea shop is wonderful!'

'Well, thank you.' Mrs Jolly and Inga exchanged glances, then Mrs Jolly said, 'Aren't you lucky to have a family who spoil you so much?'

This was something Sienna hadn't given any thought to before and it took her by surprise. But when she did think about it, Mrs Jolly was right. Inga and Matt had been looking after her exceptionally well.

'Yes, I am, Mrs Polly Jolly,' replied Sienna trying not to laugh as the funny name rolled from her lips.

'Well, I'm sure you're a good girl and show Mr and Mrs Taylor that you appreciate their kindness.'

At that moment, Sienna wasn't sure if she did or she didn't always show appreciation. All she'd been doing since she arrived at her new home was trying her best to get through each day as it came, and now her head was completely full of the mysteries of the doll's house!

So, with no answer in mind, she just smiled at Mrs Jolly. The tea shop owner smiled back before heading off to serve another customer.

As they left the tea shop, Inga asked Sienna if she wanted to go to the castle, or to the old curiosity shop that they sometimes explored, but Sienna said she was too tired, so in the end Inga took her home.

'Perhaps we'll come back later in the week when you're not so tired. Especially as you are getting into mysteries, that old curiosity shop is full of them.' But Sienna wasn't in the mood and it wouldn't be until their next visit there, that she would realise that she should have taken Inga up on her offer.

Back home, Sienna felt exhausted, so she curled up on the sofa in the lounge and slept for an hour then slouched about watching television and coloured in one of her books. The mystery of the doll's house infuriated her, and she blamed that for making her feel so sleepy. Even so, she had plans for later, and this time she would make sure she stayed awake.

In the evening Sienna said she wanted to go to bed early. Inga went upstairs with her and ran a nice relaxing lavender bubble bath, then added a splash of special lavender oil. Sienna loved bubble baths, and the sweet scent of lavender drifted through her nostrils and fired her imagination. Soon she was running through fields of purple-blue flowers with the hot summer's sun warming her olive skin. But all too soon her thoughts snapped back to reality when she remembered her plan for that night. The fields of lavender vanished.

Inga helped Sienna get ready for bed and tucked her in. Once Inga had left, Sienna set her alarm clock for midnight. Inga and Matt nearly always went to bed by eleven, so that should be a safe time to get up without disturbing them.

However, she needn't have bothered setting the alarm clock because it was piano music that woke her. She turned on her bedside lamp and looked at her clock. It was 1.30 am. Her alarm hadn't gone off and then she saw that she'd forgotten to turn the alarm switch on after setting the time. Sienna tutted in frustration at herself.

Quickly, she put on her dressing gown and slippers and crept into the playroom, where she was sure the piano music was coming from. This time she decided not to put the light on, and although the dark room was scary, she sat on the floor and listened to the music. Then, much to her annoyance, she got the feeling she was going to sneeze. She pinched the tip of her nose, she held her breath, but no matter what she did to try and stop it, she let out an enormous sneeze.

The music stopped instantly. From inside the doll's house came a scampering sound. Sienna suddenly had visions of a piano-playing, fairy-cake eating mouse. Perhaps a magic mouse? *No, that would be ridiculous.*

She stood up and turned on the light. But nothing in the room looked unusual.

'Are you a magic mouse, or a fairy?' she asked aloud. There was no response.

Sienna crouched down and stared into the music room. The piano lid was open. She was certain it had been closed before. She sat back, dumbfounded.

Just then, one of the curtains in the doll's house

bedroom twitched. Sienna jumped up in fright.

'Who's there?' Her voice sounded shaky in the silence.

No response.

'I won't harm you.'

Still no response. She was so scared her whole body shook, but she felt triumphant. There was something in the doll's house, she had proved that to herself beyond all doubt. Now she was determined to find out what it was.

7

Sienna crouched down in front of the doll's house. Gently, she opened the window where the curtain had twitched and peered inside. The room seemed empty at first glance. Then she noticed the shape of what looked like a small body under the bed cover.

'Hello,' said Sienna tentatively. 'Why don't you come out? I won't harm you; I'm your friend.' There was no response. Then, just as Sienna was about to speak again...

'I don't have any friends.' It was a girl's voice, solemn and timid.

Sienna gathered her thoughts and tried to sound calm.

'Of course you do. We all have friends somewhere. Sometimes you just need to look.'

After a few moments, the bed cover moved and a small, blonde head appeared. A little girl sat up, revealing a beautiful red dress with embroidered daisies around the neck. Sienna looked at the big blue eyes peering from underneath the girl's blonde fringe. There was something familiar about her.

'Who are you?' asked Sienna.

'I'm Anika,' said the girl.

That was not what Sienna had expected to hear, and her stomach began to churn. Had the Taylors used magic on their own daughter? 'You're Anika?' she exclaimed incredulously. 'Oh... oh, yes, of course, I've seen photographs of you. I can't believe someone put you in here!'

'No one *put* me in here. I got in by myself.'

'What? How?'

'Through the back door.'

'This doll's house doesn't have a back door!' said Sienna, confused.

'It's a magic one. I only found it by chance.'

'How did you find it?'

'Well, I was playing with the doll's house, as usual. Suddenly a little tune came into my head, so I began to hum it. Then the piano began to play the same tune. And a door appeared at the back of the house.'

'That's amazing!' said Sienna. 'What happened then?'

'Well, I walked around to have a closer look. The door got bigger and bigger, until I could just walk inside. But as soon as I went in, the door slammed shut behind me and disappeared.'

'How frightening!'

'And now I'm as small as a mouse and can't get out!'

'I don't see how you're trapped. Why don't you walk out of the front door? I'll open it for you,' offered Sienna.

'You can try, but it's never worked before.'

'In that case I'll just put my hand through the window and lift you out,' said Sienna, but as soon as her hand got close to the open window, the window slammed shut. She tried the front door, but it refused to open.

'I don't believe it!' Sienna shrieked.

'It's a horrible magic doll's house!' cried Anika,

'and I hate being trapped in here!'

Sienna kept trying to open the front door and windows, but nothing would budge. Then a thought struck her. 'What kind of tune did you hear? Perhaps if I sing it, the door will open again, and you could get out.'

'Like this,' said Anika. She hummed a little tune.

'That's the tune the piano was playing in the middle of the night!'

'Oh, that was me,' said Anika. I've been prac-
tising. I thought if I mastered it, the sound might
open the back door again so I could escape.'

'Well, let me try,' said Sienna, and she hummed
the same tune. Nothing happened. She hummed the
tune again. Then they hummed it together.

'It's useless,' said Anika. 'You're the only one who
has heard me play and seen me. Not even my mum
and dad know I'm here.'

'If they knew they would have come straight away
and rescued you!' said Sienna. 'Everyone thought
you'd run away, or that someone had kidnapped
you. Wait until I tell them you're here. They'll be
over the moon!'

Sienna ran along the corridor and swung open
the bedroom door to Inga and Matt's bedroom.

'Anika's back! Anika's back!'

Inga and Matt sat up, bleary-eyed, staring at Sienna in disbelief.

Sienna tugged at Inga's arm. 'Come on!'

Inga and Matt ran after Sienna down the corridor
and into the playroom.

'She's in there!' shouted Sienna. 'In the doll's

house!'

But even though Matt and Inga both peered into the doll's house, there was no sign of Anika. It was just an ordinary doll's house.

Inga started to cry.

Sienna stared at them. She'd never seen adults so distraught. She began to doubt herself. Had she imagined Anika being in the doll's house? Surely, she had not dreamt it all? With Inga and Matt standing there in despair before her, it all sounded absurd.

'You wicked, unkind girl!' screamed Inga. 'What a terrible trick to play on us!' She ran out of the room.

Matt gave Sienna a look she couldn't understand. Fearing he would smack her, she stepped back uncertainly and crouched behind the doll's house.

'Go to your room and stay there until we come and get you,' ordered Matt. There was a quiver in his voice, as though he was trying hard to keep control of himself. 'Use the bathroom if you need to, but I don't want you anywhere else in the house until we talk in the morning. Do you understand?'

'Yes,' muttered teary-eyed Sienna. She crept out from behind the doll's house and ran to her room, closing the door quietly behind her.

She climbed into bed and waited. She hoped that Inga or Matt would come in to say goodnight again, but no one came. Instead, she lay staring at the ceiling, wondering what the morning would bring. It was times like this that she really missed her parents. Thinking about them with a heavy heart, she reached across to the framed photograph of her and her parents, kissed them and placed it close to her chest. Then she wept.

As she cried, Sienna thought back to all the times she could have given Inga and Matt hugs, and she wished now that she had done just that, or even told them that she loved them. Seeing their sad faces made her realise just how much she did love them. It was probably too late now to say anything, because in the morning she was sure they would ask social services and to take her away, and she would have to go and live with a foster carer again.

8

It was Matt who entered Sienna's bedroom in the morning, not Inga. Sienna, fearful of the day ahead, had not slept all night.

'Get yourself washed and dressed and come down for breakfast,' said Matt, barely looking at her. When she went downstairs, she could hear Inga on the phone in the study. Sienna couldn't hear what Inga was saying through the closed door, but she was sure that Inga was talking to a social worker.

Sienna sat at the kitchen table in silence. Matt passed her a cup of tea. The only sound was the crackling of her Rice Krispies. They had never seemed so loud before.

She wasn't hungry and her stomach was churning with anxiety, but to please Matt she picked up her spoon and started to eat.

A few minutes later, Inga came in and sat at the table with them. Sienna knew it was her fault Inga looked so tired and pale. She pushed the cereal bowl away.

'Have we made you so unhappy that you want to punish us?' asked Inga.

Sienna shook her head. Tears began to trickle down her face.

'Then why make up such a terrible lie?'

There was no point telling them the truth because clearly they didn't believe her. And why should they? Nobody on earth would think her story could be true.

'I must have dreamt it,' she said, even though she knew that was a lie.

'That's what the social worker said,' said Inga. 'She thinks you've muddled up Anika's disappearance with losing your mum and dad. But you must understand that what you said was a terrible shock to us both.'

'I'm sorry,' said Sienna. 'I didn't mean to upset you. Are you going to send me away?'

'Of course not! You're our daughter. We've already lost one and we don't intend to lose another.' Inga tried to smile. 'But we don't want this to happen again.'

Sienna nodded. 'I'm really not wicked.'

'We know you're not,' said Inga. 'I'm sorry I lost my temper. It was just such a terrible shock.'

'Perhaps we should put the doll's house away for a while,' said Matt.

'Please don't do that!' cried Sienna. 'I promise I'll be good and not say another thing about the music playing and Anika being in there.'

'All right. But if you pretend Anika is in the doll's house again, we will put it away for good.'

Matt went into his study to work. He should have gone to the office, but he must have decided to stay home to keep an eye on her.

Inga brought out Sienna's favourite colouring book, full of wildlife drawings. Sienna chose a picture of a lion and began colouring it in.

But she couldn't help thinking of Anika imprisoned in the magic doll's house.

After a while, she got up and fetched her plain

sketch pad and drew Anika looking out of the doll's house window. What secrets or spells were holding her captive? If she could break the spell and rescue Anika, it would prove she hadn't been telling lies. She and Anika could become sisters and live happily together as a family. It would be wonderful.

After a while, Inga poked her head round the door. 'Perhaps you might like to play in the garden for a bit? Get some fresh air?'

Sienna didn't want to stop drawing, but neither did she want to cause any more upset, so she started to pack her pencils away.

Inga picked up the drawing of the girl in the doll's house. 'Did you draw this?'

'Yes,' replied Sienna nervously.

'Do you mind if I show this to Matt?'

'No, don't, please, it might make him angry,' pleaded Sienna.

But Inga took the drawing into Matt's office.

Sienna sat, frozen momentarily, then tip-toed to the kitchen door and out into the hallway so that she could listen to the conversation. She could just about see them through the open door to Matt's office. Scared of being seen, she waited for Matt's reaction. And when it came, it was loud; for the first time ever, she heard Matt shout.

'What the blazes is going through that girl's mind? That's it! The doll's house is going!'

His words stung and Sienna shuddered with fear. Then she heard Inga say, 'Perhaps she's testing how much we love her?'

'Seeing how upset you were last night, I'd say she's doing a fine job!' exclaimed Matt.

Inga sounded much calmer than Matt. 'Let's give the doll's house one more week, Matt. Perhaps it's helping her to work things out in her mind? We can always get rid of it if anything else happens.'

'Okay,' Matt sounded reluctant. 'If that's what you think is best.' He rubbed his chin in thought. 'Maybe you should take her out again today. Let her focus on something else.'

'I do have a little shopping I wouldn't mind getting for supper tonight,' said Inga. 'But she's not getting the delights of Jolly's tea shop, that's for sure!'

Sienna quickly tip-toed back into the kitchen, her heart beating frantically and sending waves of shivers through her body.

I've really done it this time, she thought.

9

In Richmond, the grocery shop was bustling with customers. Fruit and vegetables were stacked in neat rows, their colours vibrant. Sienna was doing her best not to get knocked by eager shoppers whilst Inga filled her basket at the other end of the shop. Suddenly, Sienna felt a sharp pinch on her arm.

'Ow!' She wheeled round to see Robbie Webster, the fiercest boy in the school, glaring at her.

'What did you do that for?' demanded Sienna.

'Felt like it,' said Robbie, with a menacing grin and a wicked glint in his eyes.

'Well, don't!'

'No girl's telling me what to do.' He pinched her again.

'Bad mistake,' whispered Sienna and stamped on his foot as hard as she could.

'Ow! She stamped on my foot!' wailed Robbie.

Sienna scuttled away, squeezing through the crowd of shoppers to find Inga. On the way, she grabbed an orange from the display. 'Can I have this?' she asked, as though nothing had happened.

'Yes,' said Inga. 'Pick another two, and we'll eat

them later.' She smiled, and Sienna felt a warm glow spread through her body.

Robbie's mother marched over, her wailing son at her side. 'Mrs Taylor, if you can't learn to supervise this child after the last one went missing, there's no hope for you at all!'

Inga stared at her in shock. Everyone in the shop fell silent. Sienna's warm glow vanished.

'I have shopping to pay for,' said Inga. She pulled Sienna to safety in front of her and marched off to the till.

'That child needs discipline!' Mrs Webster shouted as they left the shop.

Inga led Sienna away from the shop. 'Awful woman. Horrible kid,' she muttered to herself. Then she turned to Sienna and said with a smile, 'In future, don't wait to be pinched a second time,' and Sienna smiled back.

Despite what she had said to Matt earlier, Inga took Sienna to Jolly's tea shop and ordered hot chocolate with cream and luscious chocolate muffins. 'After the last few days and that horrible experience in the grocer's, I think we need as much chocolate as possible!' she said. Sienna could not disagree, and for a while the chocolate helped her forget about Anika trapped in the doll's house.

'I thought we'd have a look around the Old Curiosity Shop before we go home,' said Inga, chasing the last few chocolate crumbs around her plate.

'Oh, I'd love that!' said Sienna.

'It's where we bought that doll's house,' continued Inga.

Sienna's body went cold. She barely heard Inga continue, 'I think it would help if you had some dolls small enough to fit in there to play with.'

Sienna stared at her, horrified.

'What?' said Inga, puzzled. 'You can't have a doll's house without dolls to live in it, can you?'

'I suppose not,' said Sienna. *But what would Anika think of this*, she thought? If they got some tiny dolls to go inside, would they stay as dolls or would they come alive?

Unfortunately, this was not the only concern that sprung into Sienna's head at that precise moment. She started to wonder how she would feel if she'd been magicked away like Anika and then replaced by an adopted daughter. *Not too happy, that's for sure.*

10

The brass bell above the door clanged as Inga and Sienna entered the Old Curiosity Shop. Behind a crooked wooden table sat the owner, Mr Panagopolous, his nose buried in an exceptionally large book. Without lifting his head, he raised one eyebrow, grunted 'Good afternoon,' and cleared his throat with a cough.

'Good afternoon,' replied Inga.

Inga started to lead Anika through the shop. She seemed to know exactly where she was heading. Mr Panagopolous continued to read as if he had no interest in them, but as Sienna followed Inga, she heard a familiar tune. It was the same tune as the grand piano in the doll's house, and she was convinced Mr Panagopolous was humming it!

Inga headed deeper into the shop, but Sienna turned back to Mr Panagopolous.

'I know that tune,' exclaimed Sienna excitedly.

'What tune?' Mr Panagopolous' eyes narrowed as he looked at Sienna suspiciously.

'The one you were just humming!'

'I was singing no riddle tune,' he replied, before returning to his book.

Sienna moved closer to his desk. It was so high she had to stand on tiptoe to see over the top. The book he was reading was old and huge, full of pictures of what appeared to be gods and goddesses.

'What book is that?' she asked, trying to see more clearly. But the only thing she could get a good look at was his spiky whiskered face.

He let out a big sigh, then leaned forward and stared intently at her. At that moment, she was not sure if he was a nice man or an evil one. *Perhaps he's a wizard?* she thought.

'It's an encyclopaedia and I'm reading about Greek Mythology.'

'Oh,' said Sienna, looking rather confused.

Sienna hovered by his desk for a few moments and then in anticipation asked, 'What are riddle words?'

Mr Panagopolous raised one eyebrow and it reminded Sienna of Matt's caterpillar eyebrows.

'Well, a riddle is a collection of words, a puzzle that needs great diligence and intellect to ascertain its meaning. Why?'

'You mentioned a riddle tune, so I wanted to

know what it was.'

'I never said anything of the sort!' replied Mr Panagopolous, astounded.

'Yes, you did!' retorted Sienna.

'Young lady, if I'd said anything about riddles, I would remember. Clearly, the magic of Treasures Bright has worked its way into your imagination.'

'What's Treasures Bright?' asked Sienna.

'Now that I can help you with!' He looked up from the book and rubbed his beard. He reminded her of a scrawny elf type character she'd seen in a storybook once, but a much older version. Part of her wanted to giggle, but she thought that might insult him so he might not give her the answer. Or, worse, give her the wrong answer on purpose. So, she waited and waited. But he seemed to be in a trance.

'Mr Panagopus,' said Sienna, trying her best to get his name right. 'What's Treasures Bright?'

He snapped out of his trance and smiled at her until she feared the creases in his face would crack. 'My goodness, however do you know about Treasures Bright?'

'You just told me,' said Sienna trying not to sound rude.

'Did I? Well then, poor Mr Panagopolous is getting forgetful in his old age.' He smiled again and Sienna smiled back and decided then that she did like him.

'Treasures Bright was the name of this shop before I took it over and changed it to the Old Curiosity Shop. But that was many years ago, well before you were born.'

'Oh' said Sienna thoughtfully. She was just about to go and see what Inga was up to, when another question popped into her head.

'Why did you change the shop's name, and what kind of magic did Treasures Bright do?'

Mr Panagopolous cleared his throat again. 'Not very nice magic, from all accounts. Of course, I've only heard rumours, but I did have some very strange things happen when I first took over. That's why I changed the name; funnily enough, things have been relatively normal since then!'

Sienna was still mulling all this over in her head when Inga came over holding two miniature dolls, a tiny elderly couple. 'Do you have any small dolls apart from these?'

'Hmmm, let me think.' His face scrunched tight as he closed his eyes for a moment. 'I can't say I've seen any. Not for quite a while. But I will have a look for you.'

He got up from the chair and stretched his aching joints. 'That's the trouble with reading Greek mythology. There are so many fascinating stories, I forget how long I've been sat down. Follow me.'

He hobbled towards the rear of the shop. As she followed him, Sienna studied him carefully. He wore brown trousers, a brown jacket, and a brown checked shirt, so the bright yellow woollen socks peeping out from his enormous boots were something of a surprise, especially as they looked hand-knitted.

'What's mythlogy?' asked Sienna, almost getting the pronunciation correct.

Mr Panagopolous turned and looked at her. 'Well now. They are stories made from myths about gods and goddesses or magical beings. Like Pegasus, the flying horse. They're stories from thousands of years ago, and no one really knows if they are true. I expect you'll learn about them later in school.'

'I'm sure she will,' said Inga. 'I used to love them myself.'

'A magic myth,' said Sienna. 'Does that mean a myth is a lie?'

'Don't bother Mr Panagopolous with so many questions, Sienna,' said Inga.

'No bother,' he said. 'A myth isn't really a lie, but it's not the truth either. It's a story.' He turned away and continued towards the rear of the shop.

'Well then,' said Sienna, 'I didn't tell a lie about Anika being stuck in the doll's house, I told a story.' Inga gave her a very stern look. Sienna bit her lip and followed the grown-ups in silence.

The rear of the shop was narrow and poky, crammed with film, theatre and music memorabilia and rails of theatrical costumes, hats and jewellery. The racks of costumes gave off a musty smell which caused Sienna to wrinkle her nose.

'I can't see anything here to do with doll's houses,' said Inga.

Mr Panagopolous looked at her suspiciously. 'You

said you were looking for tiny dolls.'

'I am. To go in the doll's house we bought here.'

Mr Panagopolous became very agitated. His brow wrinkled, and he looked away from Inga. For a split second, Sienna felt his eyes ablaze on her. She wondered what he was thinking and for no reason at all, suddenly felt her face flush as if she had been naughty.

'Is there a mystery to the doll's house, then, Mr Panagopus?' asked Sienna.

'No, not that I'm aware of – but it was old stock from Treasures Bright.'

The ringing of the shop's telephone interrupted them. 'I'm sorry,' Mr Panagopolous said, 'I'll have to answer that.'

He strode off on his long gangling legs, leaving Sienna with a whirlwind of thoughts about the mystery of the doll's house and Anika trapped inside.

Inga shook her head, totally unaware of any mysteries. 'Why would he bring us back here? There's no sign of anything resembling a doll.' She took a Cinderella costume from a hook on the wall. 'This is rather nice. Perhaps you might like something like this, eh?'

Removing the costume revealed a door. Sienna rushed forward and tried the handle, but it was locked.

'Perhaps he keeps dolls in there,' said Sienna, 'but doesn't want anyone to find them.' The thought reminded her how desperately Anika needed help. She must go home. 'We can always have a look another time,' she said, and marched towards the front of the shop, leaving Inga no choice but to follow.

As Sienna passed Mr Panagopolous, who was still on the phone, something made her turn to look at him. He looked her straight in the eye and without moving his lips she heard him say, 'Dream easy, my dear girl.' Then he turned away and continued his telephone conversation as though he had not been interrupted.

Inga caught up with her and opened the shop door to let them out.

'What did he mean by "dream easy"?' asked Sienna.

'I've no idea, Sienna,' replied Inga. 'But he's talking to someone on the telephone. That's private, you shouldn't be listening!'

Not wanting to get into more trouble, Sienna followed Inga in silence back to the car.

11

Sienna lay awake until she heard the stairs creak. As soon as Matt and Inga's bedroom door clicked shut, she tiptoed out of her bedroom and into the darkness of the playroom.

'Anika,' she whispered. 'It's me, Sienna. Are you there?' There was no response. She tried again. 'Anika! Please come and talk to me. It's important!'

But Anika didn't come. Sienna gave up and crept back to bed.

She dreamed she stood outside the Old Curiosity Shop, but the name of the shop had been changed to Treasures Bright. Even though it was still night-time in her dream and very dark, the sky had a strange glow making Richmond Castle look even more haunting than usual.

Sienna raised her hand to the door handle of the shop door, but it opened at once before she even touched it. Inside, Mr Panagopolous was asleep, head down on his desk.

The eeriness of the shop unnerved her. It was as though many eyes were staring at her. Music started to play. The same tune that the piano played. Then the Cinderella costume floated away from the coat hanger and danced around her. The familiar tune made her head spin and she felt dizzy.

The Cinderella costume drifted away and transformed into the crimson dress with daisies that Anika had worn. Sienna reached out for it, but it drifted further away. She followed it, walking deeper and deeper into the shop. Then all the items in the shop drifted up into the air and changed into musical notes. They formed a swirling tunnel through which Sienna now found herself walking. As the notes swirled around her, she thought she heard Mr Panagopolous gently singing.

Through the magic door you'll hide
Until another child arrives

Only then may you be free
By broken spells from he or she

But will they know how to find
The mysteries this doll's house hides?
One clue to give you some insight
Might be to go to Treasures Bright

There inside there might just be
The mystery of a music key
Sing the riddle tune with me
And then your friend, you might set free!

Sienna ran through the tunnel of notes towards the back of the shop. BANG!

She ran smack into the locked storeroom door at the end of the shop.

'Ouch!'

She jolted awake. Looking perplexed, she checked her body over with her hands and looked around her room. She wasn't hurt at all. 'Was it a dream?' she asked herself.

Even so, she was now utterly convinced that the

key to unlock the storeroom door was some sort of magic music key.

Sienna was wide awake now, but the music she had heard in her dream was still playing, and it was coming from the playroom. She ran to the doll's house and found Anika hitting the piano keys as hard as she could.

'Where have you been?' shouted Anika. 'You just ran off and left me!' She burst into tears. It reminded Sienna of how she sobbed when she was told her parents' plane had crashed, and she started crying too.

Anika shouted, 'I've been stuck in here for days! No one bothered to come and get me, not even my mum and dad!' blubbered Anika, as she glared at Sienna through the doll's house window.

Anika wiped the tears from her face. She might be small, but when she blew her nose the noise echoed through the doll's house. 'Why are you crying? You're not stuck in here! I bet you still see your mum and dad! Why are you in my room, anyway? Who are you?'

Sienna frowned. How could she explain? She remembered all the times when adults had not been honest with her, claiming it was 'for her own good,' and decided the best way was to come straight out with it.

'I'm Sienna. I'm your new sister.'

'Mum and dad have had a baby since I got stuck in here? But you're old!'

'I'm not old, I'm only just seven! My birthday was on February the fifth.'

'What day is it now?' asked Anika.

'Tenth of August.'

'What year?' asked Anika.

Sienna hesitated. 'Well, you've been gone for an awfully long time.'

'Not long enough for them to get another sister for me!' Anika pulled up a chair and sat by the window. 'When you're stuck in here for days, it feels like years – I NEED TO GET OUT!'

Sienna felt miserable for her and didn't know what to say. So she stayed silent and listened to Anika continue.

'What happened when you told my parents you'd found me? Why didn't they come and get me?'

With bated breath, Sienna solemnly and reluctantly mumbled, 'They didn't believe me.'

12

Sienna and Anika sat in silence. She wondered how it would feel to be magicked away and replaced by an adopted daughter. Pretty awful, she was sure.

'I don't know how I'm ever going to be free,' Anika said after a while. 'If mum and dad didn't believe you, I've got no chance.'

Sienna tried pushing the front door of the doll's house open again.

'That's no use,' grumbled Anika. 'Each time I get close to the front door, I hit an invisible barrier and it's the same with the windows.'

'I'll get something sharp and break the barrier down.' Sienna started to get up.

'No,' said Anika. 'This is a magic doll's house. When I first got in here a voice warned that if I didn't leave the same way I came in, I would be lost forever.'

Sienna sat down again. 'I never really believed in magic,' she said. 'How wrong I was!'

'Oh, magic exists all right. Look at me. Stuck in here like Thumbelina, no bigger than a thimble!' Anika stomped her way around the downstairs of the doll's house marched upstairs and throw herself onto her bed and wept.

'It's no use,' she wailed, 'The magic is too power-ful. I'm never going to be free!' Anika put her head in her hands, sobbing.

Sienna sat back, exhausted. If she fetched Inga or Matt, they wouldn't believe her and think she'd made up another nasty lie. She would be sent away, and Anika might be lost forever.

'I think Mr Panagopus from the Old Curiosity Shop has something to do with this,' said Sienna. 'All his nonsense about riddle tunes and songs even got me dreaming about magic keys and musical notes!'

Snotty nosed and red-eyed Anika jumped off the bed and rushed over to the window. 'But what if your dream is true? What if he holds the secret to set me free?' Her shoulders slumped and she took out a handkerchief from her pocket and wiped her eyes and nose. 'Why would he want to lock me in here? I thought he was a lovely old man, even though he didn't want mum to buy this doll's house.'

Sienna's eyes narrowed, like a detective suddenly finding a clue to solve a crime. 'He didn't want to sell you the doll's house?'

'No, he didn't, he kept trying to tempt mamma with other toys and costumes, things that are no good at all when you're the only child.'

Sienna's heart leapt at the thought of them dressing up and playing together. 'I can't wait until you get out and we can play together and become proper sisters!'

'Oh, do think of a way to get me out of here! I promise I won't be angry at mum and dad for having another baby and forgetting about me, even if you must have been born BIG!'

Sienna gazed through the window at Anika, who wandered back to the bed and perched on the edge with a sad, defeated look on her face. There was no escaping it. She would have to explain. 'Your mother and father didn't have another baby like they had you, Anika. They adopted me a few years after my mum and dad died. But I was never meant to replace you. I think they just wanted to help another child.'

Anika looked shocked. 'I'm sorry you lost your mum and dad. You must feel really sad. At least I still have mine.' She looked up at Sienna, who moved closer to the doll's house and touched the windows gently with her fingers.

'I don't mind sharing my mamma and papa with you. Not if we're going to be sisters. I think I'd really like that,' said Anika.

Sienna smiled. 'Oh, I do hope we can make this happen!' She rubbed her tired eyes. For the first time since her parents died, she felt a real sense of love. Although she still felt sad, Anika's words moved her so much that her tears were also tears of joy.

13

'But I need to see Mr Panagopus!' shouted Sienna as Inga put porridge in front of her next morning. 'I don't want to walk on the moors.'

Inga sighed. 'Why would you want to visit a cranky old man rather than hike across the moors and see all the wildlife?'

'I just do!' Sienna pushed her porridge away.

'All right,' said Inga. 'We'll go to the shop first then visit the park on the way home. A bit of fresh air will do us both good.'

Sienna shovelled down her porridge as though she hadn't eaten for a week. The sooner she finished breakfast, the sooner she could solve the mystery of the doll's house.

The big brass bell seemed even louder than last time as they opened the door to the Old Curiosity Shop.

Mr Panagopolous was not at his desk. Inga looked around the empty shop. 'He's not even here. What did you want to see him about?'

Sienna hadn't thought about what she was going to say to Mr Panagopolous. She felt stupid for not thinking it through. Then an idea came to her. 'I wanted to try on the Cinderella costume.'

Inga shook her head, smiling. 'You could have just asked. Come on, then – I'm sure he won't mind.' She walked towards the rear of the shop followed by Sienna, who was wondering why she hadn't written down the words of the riddle song from her dream. *If only I could remember.* Quietly, she began to hum the tune, adding what words she could recall.

Only then may you be free
By broken spells from he or she
The mysteries this doll's house hides?

No, that wasn't right. She felt annoyed with herself for not being able to remember.

'That's a strange little tune,' said Inga. 'Where did you learn that?'

'I must have just heard it somewhere.'

Just then the words of the riddle song echoed through the shop, sung by Mr Panagopolous, and Sienna found herself joining in.

There inside there might just be
The mystery of a music key
Sing the riddle tune with me
And then your friend, you might set free!

'Very nice singing, Sienna,' said Inga.

Sienna couldn't understand why Inga hadn't heard Mr Panagopolous singing too. *'I mean, if it's not Mr Panagopus singing the riddle tune, then who else could it be?'* she muttered to herself.

Inga found the Cinderella costume, lifted it down and held it up against Sienna. 'I think this'll fit, but you'd better try it on just to make sure.' She looked around the shop. 'I wonder where Mr Panagopolous has got to?'

'He's in that cupboard, singing,' said Sienna, pointing to the locked door behind them.

'Don't be silly,' said Inga, laughing. 'The only person singing this morning is you, and I have to admit you have a very lovely voice!'

Sienna blushed, embarrassed. It was the first time she had sung loudly like that since her parents died, so Inga had never heard her sing at all.

'Come on, try this for size.' Inga went to slip the dress over Sienna's head but at that very moment, Sienna spotted a large sparkling key sticking out from the store cupboard's keyhole. She dashed over and grabbed the key, shoving it into the pockets of her shorts.

'Sienna! What are you doing?' said Inga laughing.

'Oh, nothing. I thought that cupboard was open. I wanted to take a look.'

Sienna rattled the door handle, with one hand whilst the other firmly held the key in her pocket. But then she realised just how big the key was. *How am I going to smuggle this out without anyone seeing?* she thought. Then another idea quickly sprang to mind.

Just at that moment, the shop bell rang, and Mr Panagopolous bellowed, 'Hello! Have I got customers somewhere?'

Inga called out, 'We're in the back, Mr Panagopolous!'

'I just popped out for a pint of milk,' replied Mr Panagopolous.

Sienna knew she had to act fast, so she snatched the Cinderella dress from Inga and slipped it over her head and T-shirt as quickly as she could. *This will hide the key sticking out of my shorts,* she thought.

'Sienna! Now look what you've done!' exclaimed Inga.

Mr Panagopolous walked towards them but then stopped and roared with laughter.

Sienna's head was entirely hidden by the Cinderella costume and her arms stuck awkwardly in the air. In her panic, she had put the dress on back to front.

'I can't move!' squealed Sienna, almost toppling over.

'I see that!' said Mr Panagopolous, still laughing

uncontrollably.

'Stand still, Sienna,' said Inga. 'You didn't unzip the back of the dress.' She steadied Sienna and unzipped the dress, revealing a red-faced Sienna underneath. Fortunately, as she helped Sienna out of the dress and put it on the right way round, the key had worked itself into the lining of her shorts through a hole in her pocket.

'Perfect!' said Inga. 'We'll take this, Mr Panagopolous.'

'Right,' said Mr Panagopolous. I'll just get you a new one from the stockroom.'

'Oh, no!' shouted Sienna. 'Can't I have this one now I've got it on? I'd like to wear it home.'

Even though the key might not be visible in her shorts, she did not want to risk it being discovered.

'Oh, my goodness, Sienna, you are acting rather strangely today,' said Inga.

'Would that be okay, Mr Panagopolous?' asked Inga.

He walked over to the door from which Sienna had removed the sparkling key. All the time, Sienna's suspicious eyes were fixed on him.

'That's the magic of the stock room,' he said, then winked. 'You never know what exciting things you might find in there!'

He looked at Sienna, thoughtfully. 'Is that the Cinderella dress you want, young lady?' Sienna's head was spinning, the best she could do was to nod 'yes'. Mr Panagopolous smiled, then walked away to the front of the shop.

Just then the words of the riddle song echoed through the shop and it sounded very much like Mr Panagopolous, and suddenly, Sienna found herself remembering the words and joining in.

There inside there might just be
The mystery of a music key
Sing the riddle tune with me
And then your friend, you might set free!

But when Inga and Sienna got to the front of the shop to pay Mr Panagopolous, he wasn't singing at all. Instead he was writing out a receipt for the Cinderella dress purchase.

'This is a magical mystery shop!' stated Sienna as

Inga led her out of the shop after paying for the dress.

'Sometimes, Sienna Taylor, I have no idea what's going in your mind at all!' Inga gave her a wide smile.

Sienna did a twirl in the street and her Cinderella dress whirled out around her, 'Neither do I!' she replied, and they both laughed.

14

Sienna rushed upstairs to her bedroom still wearing her Cinderella dress. Quickly, she lifted up the dress and removed the key from her shorts. She looked at it in horror. There was no sparkle to the key at all. It was just plain and ordinary.

'Oh no!' she cried. 'The magic has gone, and now I won't ever be able to rescue Anika!'

She threw the key into her rubbish bin and wished now that she had asked Mr Panagopolous about the key and the magic stockroom. She had wasted the entire day!

Sienna went to bed exhausted that night and fell asleep instantly.

It was dawn when the piano music woke her from her dreams about the riddle song and the Old Curiosity Shop. Her curtains were still open, so she walked to the window and watched the glow of the early sunrise. How wonderful it was!

Still tired from yesterday and wondering what she was going to say to Anika, she put on her slippers and dressing gown and went to the playroom. There, Anika was waiting at the window, peering out in anticipation.

'What took you so long? I've been waiting ages! Did you speak to Mr Panapolous?' asked Anika, also pronouncing his name wrong. 'Have you solved the mystery of the riddle song?' blurting all the questions out one after the other without giving Sienna a chance to respond.

But all Sienna could do was to look at the floor and mumble, 'Sorry.' She slumped to the floor and told Anika everything that had happened, or rather hadn't happened, and how sorry she was that she had failed her mission.

Anika felt sorry for Sienna. 'At least you tried! Why don't you bring the key in here and let me look at it?'

'Okay,' said Sienna. But when she bent down to

pick the key up from the rubbish bin in her bed-room, the key had disappeared. In its place she dis-covered a gold envelope with tiny daisies decorating its edges.

Puzzled, she took the envelope back to the play-room. 'I don't understand. The key has gone but I've found this. It's very pretty but...'

'Quick! Open it! It might be magic!' urged Anika.

'Of course, it's not magic!' said Sienna.

'But the daisies on the envelope are just like the ones on my dress! Don't you think that means something?'

With little enthusiasm, Sienna opened the envelope and pulled out a folded piece of paper. When she opened it her eyes bulged with excitement. 'It's the words to the riddle song!'

'Read it out loud!' squealed Anika excitedly.

Sienna read the riddle song, but the doors of the doll's house didn't open. Sienna read it again, but still nothing happened.

'I hate riddle songs!' Sienna angrily screwed up the piece of paper and threw it on the floor.

'That's it!' shouted Anika. 'It's a riddle SONG! You're not supposed to read it. You're supposed to sing it!'

She rushed to the piano and started the play the tune. Sienna picked up the piece of paper, smoothed it out and begun to sing the words to the piano music Anika was playing.

Through the magic door, you'll hide
Until another child arrives

Only then may you be free
By broken spells from he or she

But will they know how to find
The mysteries this doll's house hides?
One clue to give you some insight
Might be to go to Treasures Bright

There inside there might just be
The mystery of a music key
Sing the riddle tune with me
And then your friend, you might set free!

The moment she stopped singing Sienna heard a cough. She turned to see Matt and Inga in the doorway both looking flabbergasted.

'What are you doing, Sienna? It's six o'clock in the morning.'

Without thinking, Sienna replied, 'I'm singing the Treasures Bright riddle song to set Anika free.'

But the piano music had stopped. And when Sienna looked into the doll's house, Anika was nowhere to be seen. Sienna's heart pounded. Inga and

Matt would never believe her now – or forgive her.

The three of them stared at one another, unable to speak.

Suddenly the front doorbell rang, and Matt snapped out of the silence. 'Who on earth could it be at this time in the morning? Stay here, you two. I'll sort out this nonsense once I've sorted out who's at the door!'

But inquisitive Inga and Sienna followed Matt downstairs and watched him unbolt and open the door. 'Oh...!' he gasped and stepped back in amazement. There, standing in the doorway was a normal-sized Anika, staring up at him.

'Hello, Papa,' Anika said.

Matt's legs buckled in shock. But as he fell to his knees, he opened his arms to embrace his long-lost daughter.

'Anika?' called Inga, her lips quivering. 'Anika!' Inga rushed over, and all three of them hugged and kissed, and wept.

Sienna watched the emotional reunion. This was how her mum and dad would greet her if they were ever reunited, and the thought of her parents made her start to cry.

So many thoughts rushed through her head that she could hardly breathe. Despite her deep sadness that she could never greet her own parents this way again, she felt such joy seeing Anika with her mum and dad, all together again. She felt proud of herself too. After all, she had helped to set Anika free.

But now that Matt and Inga had their birth daughter back, perhaps they wouldn't want her to stay. This final thought overwhelmed her, and she fainted.

Sienna woke to find herself lying on the settee in the lounge with a cold cloth covering her forehead, muttering. 'It's not Mr Panagopus's fault, it's Treasures Bright.'

Inga leaned over her and removed the cloth from her forehead.

'Just stay there for a while longer, darling,' said Inga and gently kissed her on the forehead. 'Everything is going to be okay. The doctor is here, just checking Anika over.'

'Anika?' said Sienna, confused.

'Yes, Sienna. Your sister has come home.'

'Yes, I know mamma, isn't it just the most wonderful thing that could ever have happened!'

Sienna sat up and gave Inga the biggest hug she had ever given anyone in her entire life – and then Anika ran over and hugged her too!

But would this be the end of their adventures?

Well, we will just have to wait and see...

Did you enjoy this book?

If so, please talk to an adult member of your family or carer and ask them to help you write a brief review and give the book a star rating on Amazon website. But remember not to give away any of the story's secrets away as this will ruin the read for other children.

Writing a review or even giving the book a star rating can help an author enormously and authors love to hear from their readers!

Until the next time – **THANK YOU!**

Jean Maye

Mouse Chased Cat
Publications

ABOUT THE AUTHOR

Writing/Author website address:
www.jeanmayeauthor.com

Jean is an international best-selling author for children's workbooks in relation to fostering and adoption. She is also a multi-award-winning screenwriter. Her screen-writing accolades can be seen on her screenwrit-ing/film's website: www.mousechasedcat.com

Jean's writing skills are supported by a varied range of qualifications including a master's degree in Creative Writing at Kingston University in 2012, a summer course at Oxford University plus many other writing forums and conferences.

THE DOLLS HOUSE is her first children's fiction novel.

www.jeanmayeauthor.com
facebook.com/mccpress
Twitter @jean_maye
Instagram @jeanmaye
Linkedin - jean-maye-05243120

Mouse Chased Cat
Publications